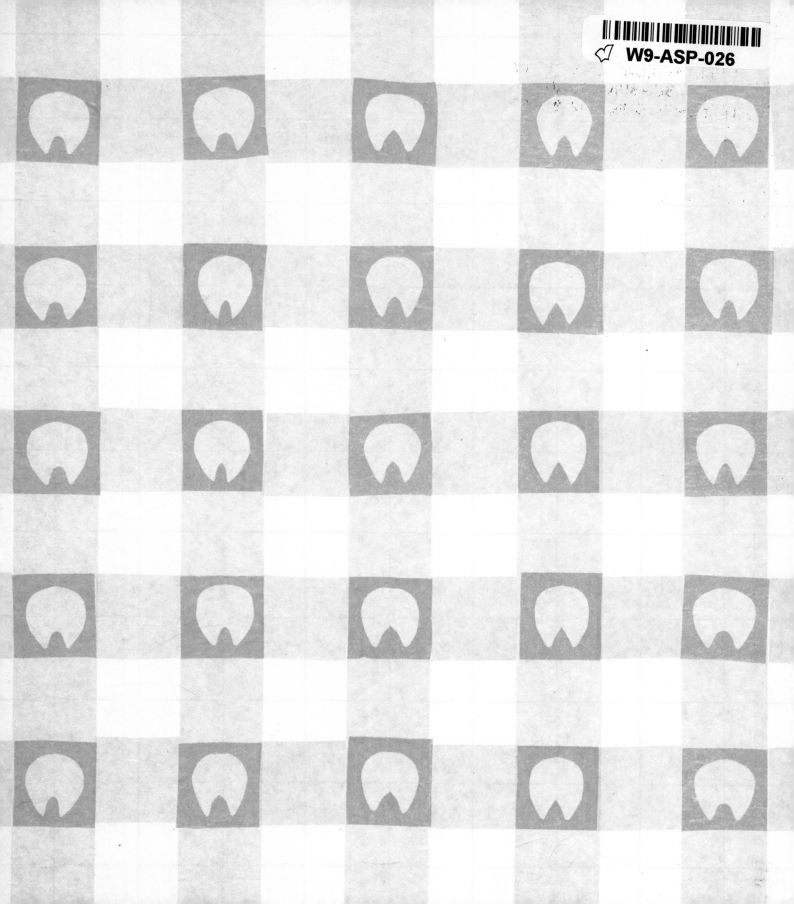

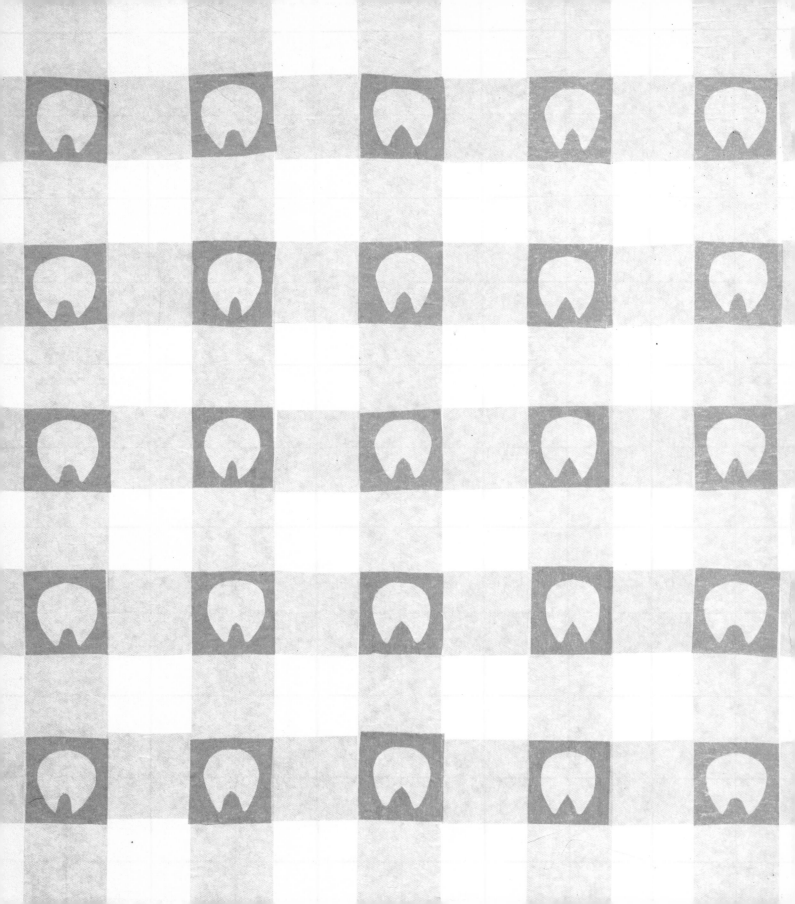

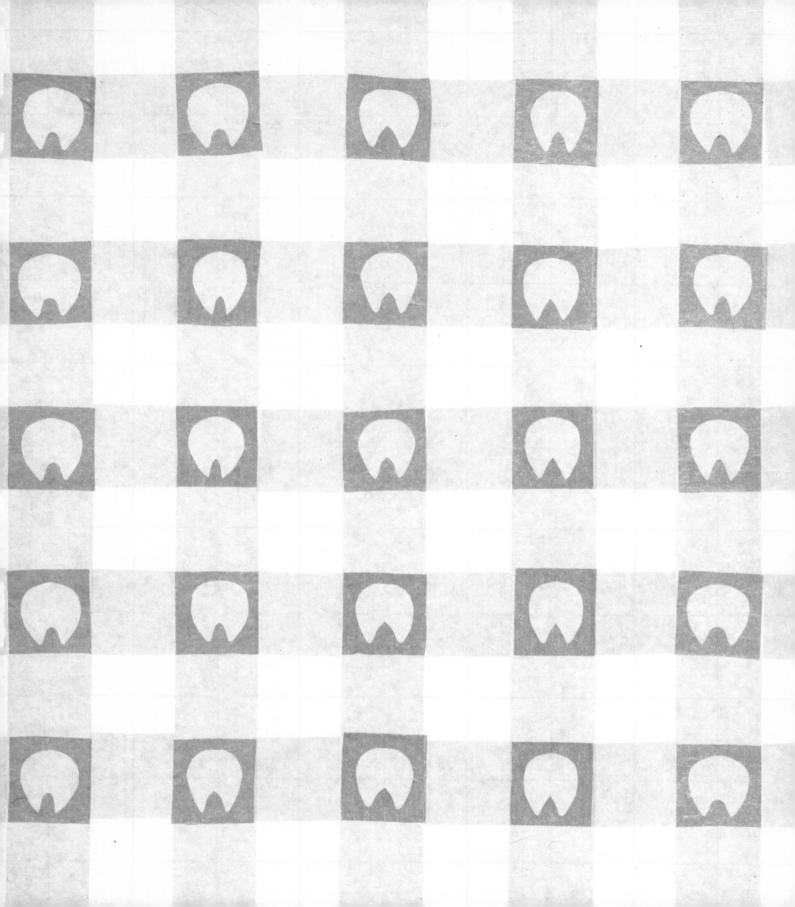

Alice and Her Fabulous Teeth

Robin Maconie

art by

Catherine Myler Fruisen

Cedco Publishing • San Rafael, California

ISBN 0-7683-2176-X

Text copyright © Robin Maconie
Illustrations by Catherine Myler Fruisen
Art copyright © 1999 Design Press Books
All rights reserved.

Published in 2000 by Cedco Publishing Company.
100 Pelican Way, San Rafael, California 94901
For a free catalog of other Cedco® products, please write to the address
above, or visit our website: www.cedco.com

Book and jacket design by Janice Shay

This is a Design Press Book.
Design Press is a division of the Savannah College of Art and Design.

Printed in China

1 3 5 7 9 10 8 6 4 2

*This book is dedicated
to my dear daughter Alys
who has her Mother to thank
for her truly fabulous teeth.*

Let me tell you the story
of Alice's teeth,
The most talked about gnashers
of Blueberry Heath.

And if you are wondering
where she has got 'em—
There are ten
on the top—
And ten more
on the bottom.

She looked after her choppers,
  she brushed them with care;
She trained them on apple,
  and carrot, and pear,
And not many cookies,
  or chocolates, or sweets,
  For teeth don't take kindly
  to sugary treats.

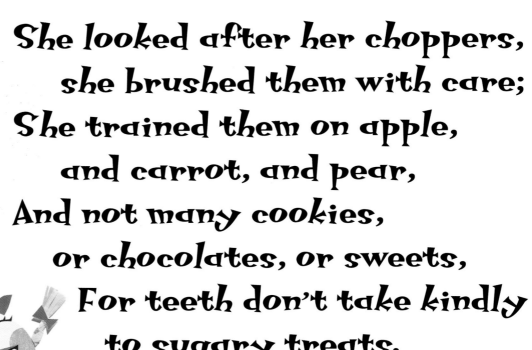

Now teeth are important,
  I think you should know;
They allow you to talk,
  and they help you to grow.

If you haven't got teeth,
  you can't whistle or bite;
There is nothing to brush
  before bedtime at night.

If you haven't got teeth,
   you can't chew up your food!
You have to go "sluurp!"
   with a spoon—
         which is rude!

If you haven't got teeth, it's not easy to say

"Twenty-three Pterodactyls tapdancing today."

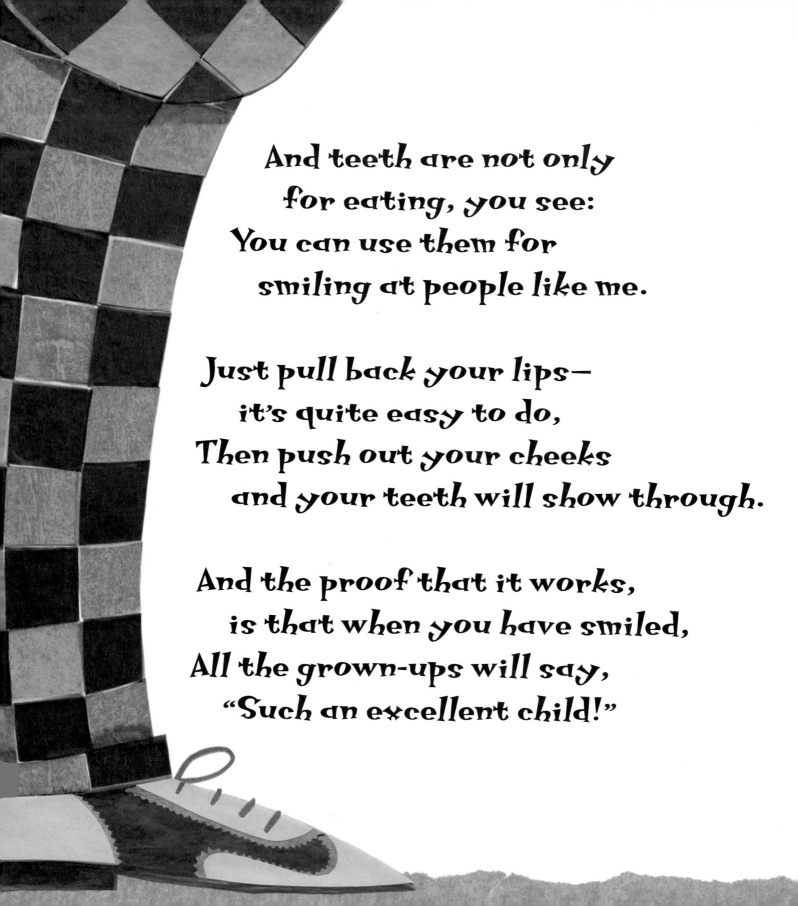

And teeth are not only
for eating, you see:
You can use them for
smiling at people like me.

Just pull back your lips—
it's quite easy to do,
Then push out your cheeks
and your teeth will show through.

And the proof that it works,
is that when you have smiled,
All the grown-ups will say,
"Such an excellent child!"

Now, when she was young Alice happened to go
Two or three times a year, to the Dentist, to show
Him her fabulous teeth, and how healthy they were.
And the Dentist would settle her down in a chair.

Then the Dentist would say, "Alice, please open wide!
And we'll see just how many are growing inside."
So Alice said "Ahhh!" and the Dentist said "Hey!
Your teeth are superb! Kindly sign this X-ray!"

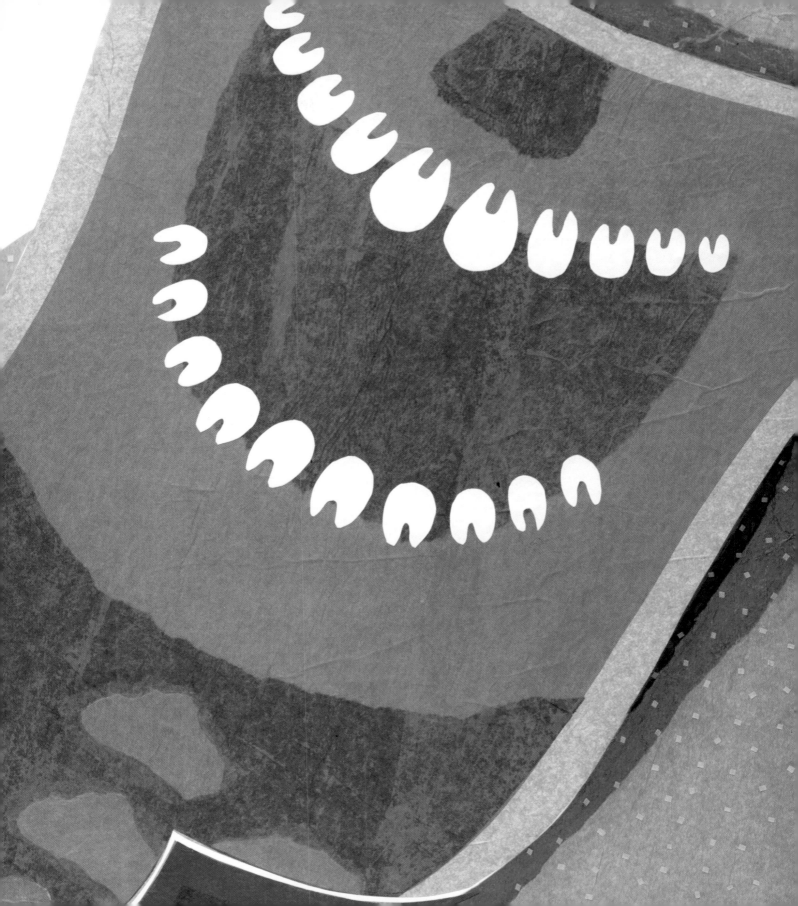

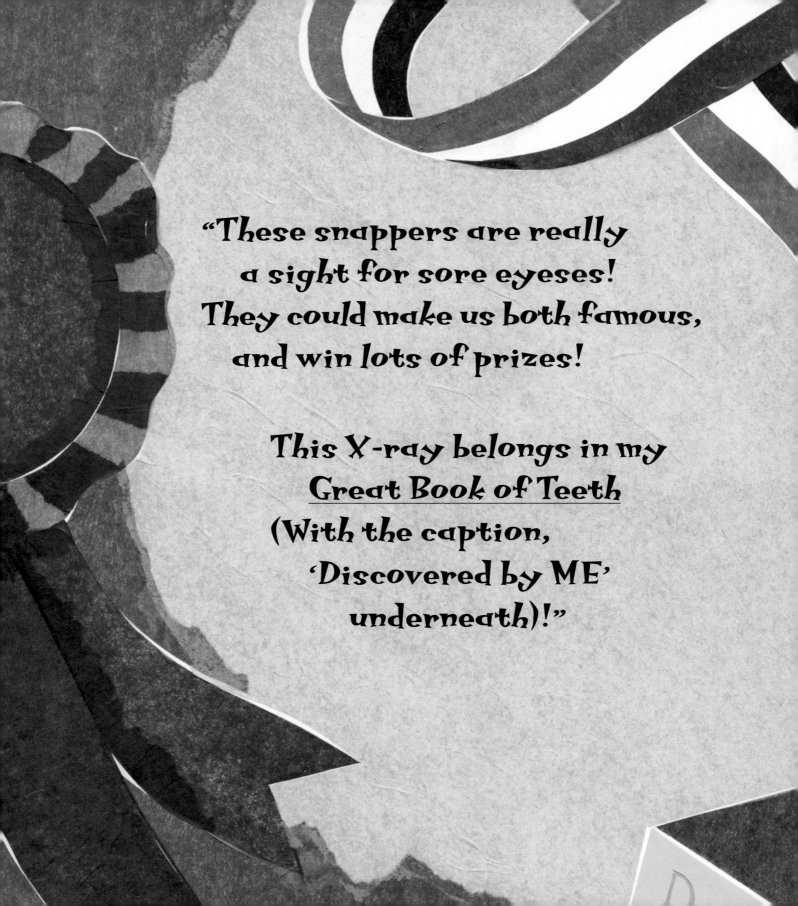

"These snappers are really
a sight for sore eyeses!
They could make us both famous,
and win lots of prizes!

This X-ray belongs in my
Great Book of Teeth
(With the caption,
'Discovered by ME'
underneath)!"

But Alice was smart.
    She was nobody's fool.
She could tell from the smiles of
    the children at school
That her baby teeth one day
    would loosen and go
To make room for a new set of
    choppers to grow.

The question was this:
    Could she quickly grow more,
If they suddenly happened
    to fall on the floor—
When she sneezed rather loudly,
    or started to sing—
Like a necklace of beads that have
    broken their string?

Now when a tooth loosens, the way that you know
Is by biting on food. When you feel something go
There's a vague kind of squelch, and a squinge,
    And a squoze,
Which is rather like biting an old rubber hose.

And it doesn't feel right,
    though it's not at all sore.
Then your tongue tries to push it
    around in your jaw
And you just keep on trying
    to push to and fro
On the newly-loose tooth
    that's beginning to go.

And she fussed with the tooth,
    till it started to wobble
And her teacher said,
    "Alice, just what is the trouble?"

"It's my tooth," Alice said,
    "It's distracting, I know.
But what else can one do
    when one's tooth has to go?"

And she pointed to where
    the unfortunate hung,
And wiggled and wobbled it
    more with her tongue.

That evening—at last—
　　It came out in a lump!
A great ivory peg
　　with a red-colored stump!

　　And her Mommy said,
　　　"Rinse it, and make it all white
　　If you want the tooth fairy
　　　to visit tonight!"

So she washed it, and dried it,
　　and Oh! how it gleamed!
Put it under her pillow…

...and that night
she dreamed
Of conducting an
auction of
nearly-new choppers
In front of a roomful of
Fairyland shoppers.

"Now what will you give,"
    she could hear herself ask,
"For this perfect, original ivory tusk?"
(Holding up her lost tooth)
    "Do I hear thirty-three?
Thirty-five is a bargain,
    I'm sure you'll agree."

And the bidding began, with the pixies and elves
All deciding they wanted the tooth for themselves.

So the price kept on rising—now sixty, now more,
As the bids thick and fast
    crossed the auction-room floor.
Till a voice loud and clear said,
    "Enough of this riot!
I'm the Tooth Fairy here, and I'm going to buy it!"

And the rest of the fairies fell suddenly quiet
As she lifted the tooth up
    and started to eye it,
And said, "It's the best! I won't try to deny it.
Just tell me how much,
    'Cause I really must dash.
By the way, would you rather
    take plastic or cash?"

But before she could say, Alice woke with a start
And a gleam in her eye, and a thump in her heart,
And lifting her pillow, saw the fairy had brought her
Two dollars, four nickels, three dimes and a quarter!

Which just goes to show that
whatever the size is,
If you treat your teeth well,
they will fetch the best prices.

(And that's the tooth!)

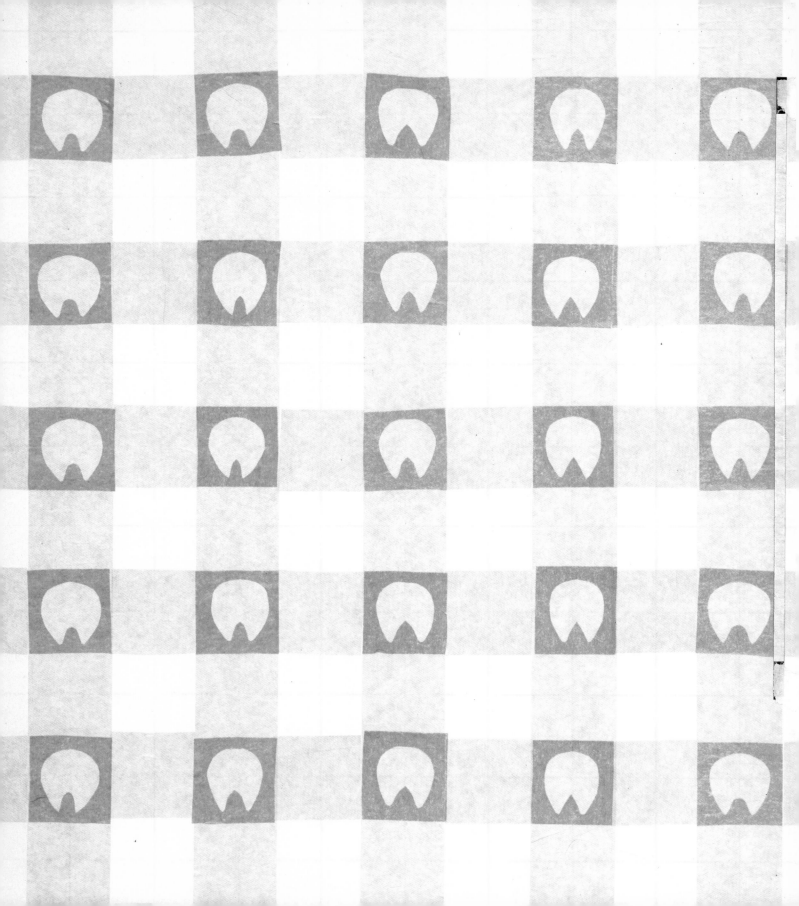

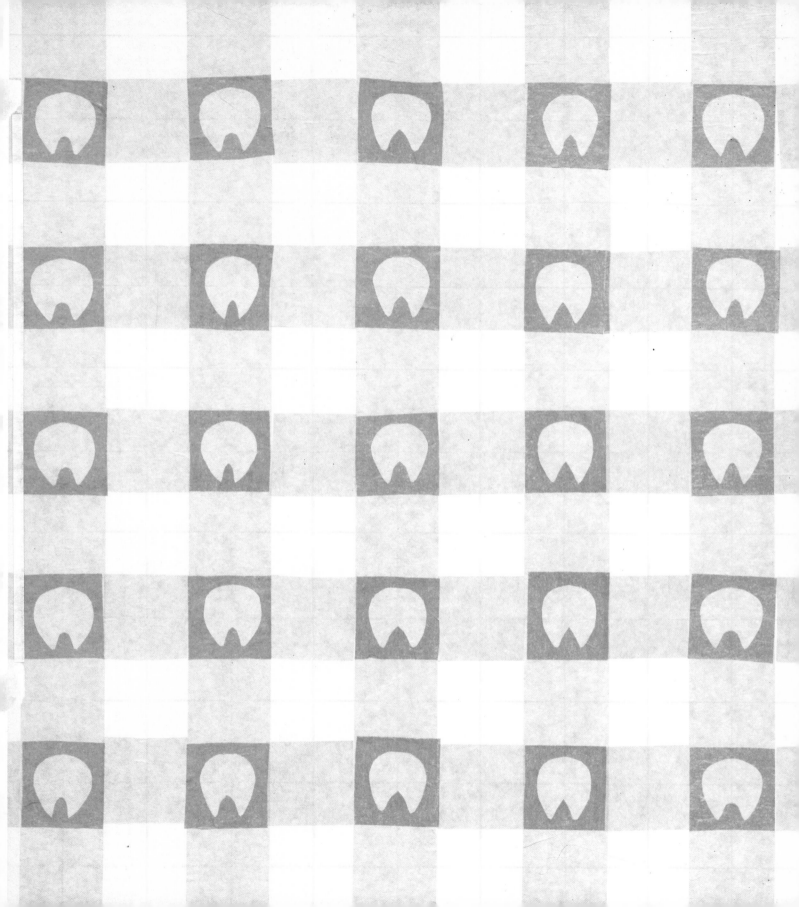

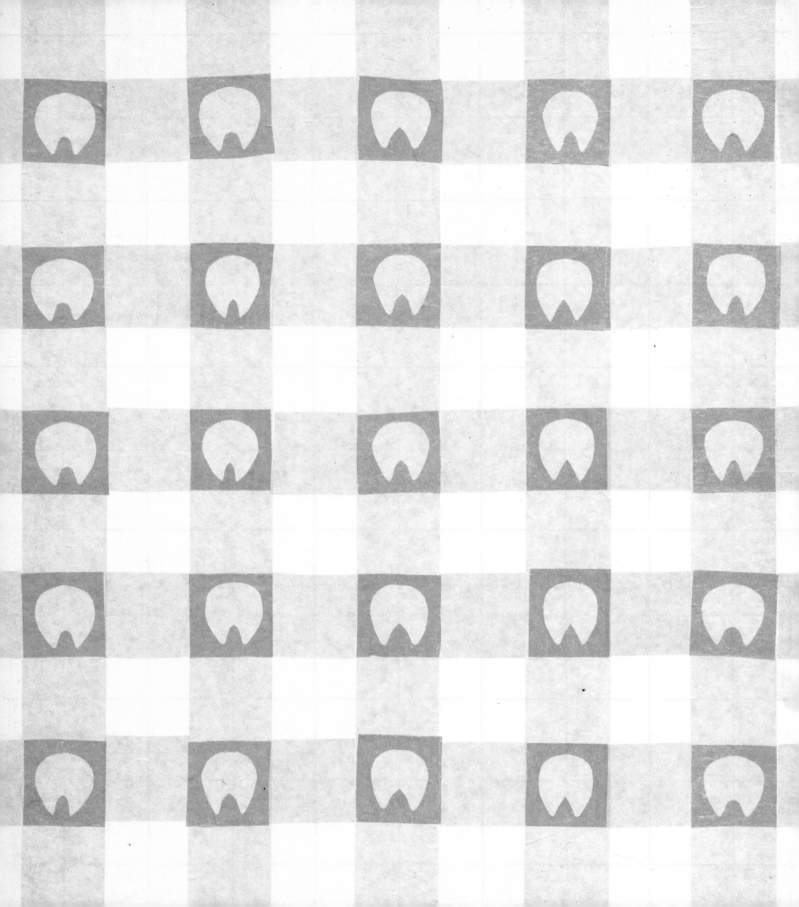